DRAW!

Raúl Colón

A Paula Wiseman Book

SIMON & SCHUSTER BOOKS FOR YOUNG READERS

New York   London   Toronto   Sydney   New Delhi

For Joan, a white butterfly in the sky

SIMON & SCHUSTER BOOKS FOR YOUNG READERS
An imprint of Simon & Schuster Children's Publishing Division
1230 Avenue of the Americas, New York, New York 10020
Copyright © 2014 by Raúl Colón
All rights reserved, including the right of reproduction in whole or in part in any form.
SIMON & SCHUSTER BOOKS FOR YOUNG READERS is a trademark of Simon & Schuster, Inc.
For information about special discounts for bulk purchases, please contact Simon & Schuster
Special Sales at 1-866-506-1949 or business@simonandschuster.com.
The Simon & Schuster Speakers Bureau can bring authors to your live event. For more information
or to book an event, contact the Simon & Schuster Speakers Bureau at 1-866-248-3049 or visit our
website at www.simonspeakers.com.
Book design by Laurent Linn
The illustrations for this book are rendered in pen and ink, watercolors, Prismacolor pencils,
and lithograph pencils on Arches paper.
Manufactured in China
0514 SCP
2 4 6 8 10 9 7 5 3 1
Library of Congress Cataloging-in-Publication Data
Colón, Raúl, author, illustrator.
Draw! / Raúl Colón ; illustrated by Raúl Colón.
pages cm
"A Paula Wiseman Book."
Summary: In this wordless picture book, a boy who is confined to his room fills his sketch pad
with lions and elephants, then imagines himself on a safari.
ISBN 978-1-4424-9492-3 (hardcover) — ISBN 978-1-4424-9493-0 (eBook)
[1. Drawing—Fiction. 2. Imagination—Fiction. 3. Safaris—Fiction. 4. Animals—Fiction.
5. Stories without words.] I. Title.
PZ7.C716365Dr 2014
[E]—dc23
2013043781

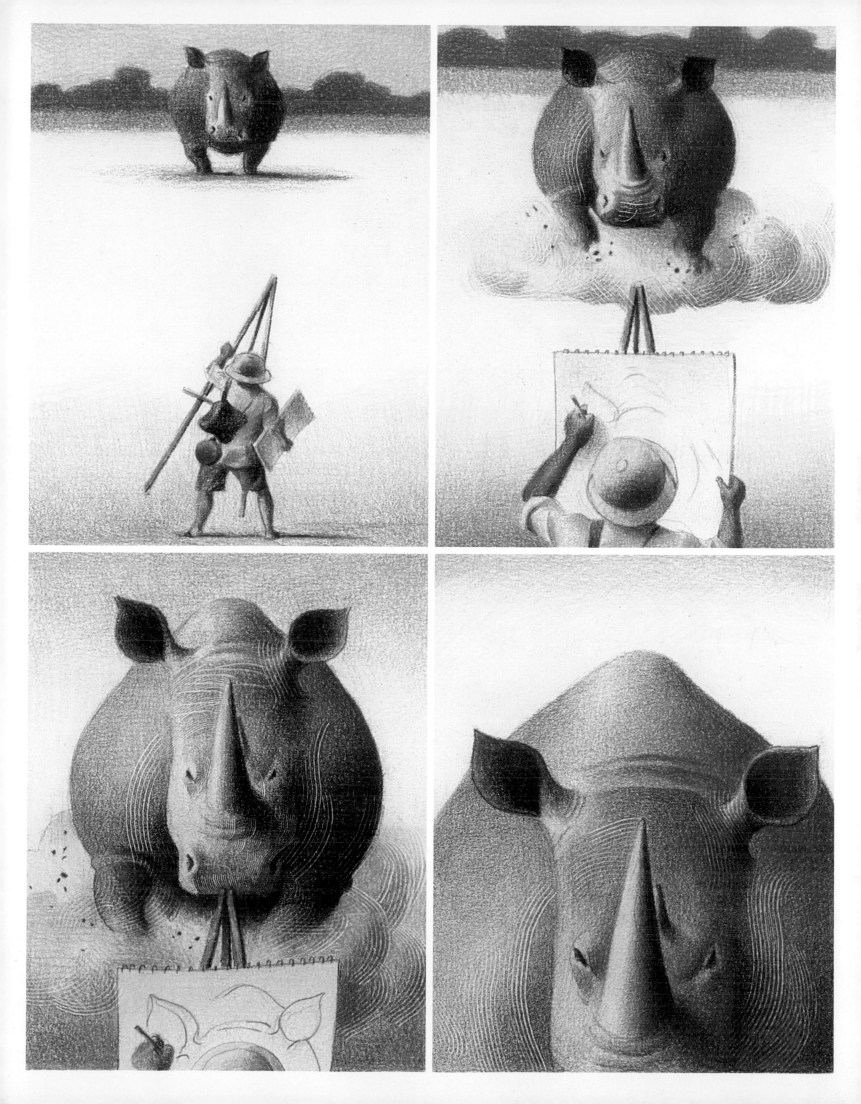

AUTHOR'S NOTE

When I was growing up in New York City, I would often stay in my room, where I would spend long hours drawing. When I drew, I could go anywhere my imagination led me. These many happy times were the inspiration for *Draw!* My parents were avid readers and I always had books, from the Bible and classics to magazines and even comic books, that fueled the images in my brain. Artists like Norman Rockwell, Steve Ditko (the original illustrator for Spider-Man), Joe Kubert, and others became my teachers, so to speak, as I tried to learn how they put their images on paper. I used up dozens and dozens of composition notebooks trying to draw and even write my own stories. When I ran out of paper my older sister's school notebooks came in handy. I talked her into handing them over when she was asked to babysit me by making a deal that allowed her to secretly go out and play with her friends while I drew away in our apartment.

When I grew older and moved to Puerto Rico I discovered other artists, such as the impressionists, surrealists, and finally contemporary illustrators. In high school I took a course on commercial art with a great teacher, Mr. Victor Cortez. Eventually, after years of paying my dues, I started my freelance illustration career and returned to the Big Apple.

Another facet of my work I've enjoyed is the pleasure of teaching other young aspiring artists about the principles of illustration and seeing them develop their own careers. The aha moment for *Draw!* came after I saw a great exhibit titled *Ashes and Snow* by the photographer Gregory Colbert. It was aptly described as a "symphony of animals." By blending the visuals of life in the wild with my childhood memories, I dreamed up the images in this book. Now I hope these images inspire others to have their very own dreams, and just draw—draw away.

—RAÚL COLÓN